Playing with Gravity

Published in the United States of America by Cherry Lake Publishing
Ann Arbor, Michigan
www.cherrylakepublishing.com

Reading Adviser: Marla Conn MS, Ed., Literacy specialist, Read-Ability, Inc.
Book Design: Jennifer Wahi
Illustrator: Jeff Bane

Library of Congress Cataloging-in-Publication Data has been filed and is available at catalog.loc.gov

Printed in the United States of America
Corporate Graphics

About the illustrator: Jeff Bane and his two business partners own a studio along the American River in Folsom, California, home of the 1849 Gold Rush. When Jeff's not sketching or illustrating for clients, he's either swimming or kayaking in the river to relax.

Science Notes

Playing with Gravity explores how gravity affects objects of different sizes. In this experiment, the reader drops a large ball and a small ball and compares how much time it takes for them to hit the ground. The time should be the same or very close.

Jump! You go up. Then you come down. This is because of **gravity.** Gravity keeps things close to the earth.

When have you felt gravity working?

Does gravity **affect** big and small things differently?

Let's find out!

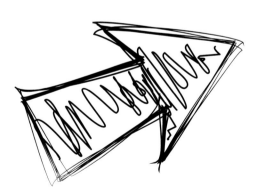

- Parent or friend to help
- Chair
- Big ball (soccer ball or basketball)
- **Timer**
- Paper
- Pencil
- Small ball (golf ball or baseball)

You will need these things

Have your parent or friend stand on the chair. Be careful!

Will this work without a chair?
Why or why not?

Ask your helper to drop the big ball.

Start the timer when it drops. Stop the timer when it hits the ground.

Write down the time.

Do it again with the small ball.

Write down the time.

Did the balls bounce?
Do you know why?

Compare the two times.

Your times should be very close.

Drop both balls at the same time. You will see them hit the ground together.

Why do you think this is?

Try it with a book. Try it with a water bottle.

Try it with an apple!

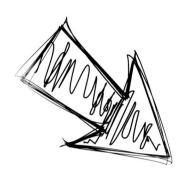

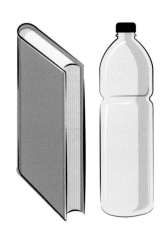

Good job. You're done!
Science is fun!

What new questions do you have?

glossary

affect (uh-FEKT) to cause something to happen

compare (kuhm-PAIR) to look at two things closely to see how they are the same and different

gravity (GRAV-ih-tee) the force that pulls things toward the center of the earth and keeps them from floating away

timer (TIME-ur) something that keeps track of a period of time

index